To our good friend, Hisako,
from Eric and Kazuo.

Copyright © 2001 by Eric Carle and Kazuo Iwamura
First published in Japan in 2001 by Doshin-sha Publishing Co.

LIBRARY OF CONGRESS CATALOGING-IN-PUBLICATION DATA

Carle, Eric.
Where are you going? To see my friend! / Eric Carle & Kazuo Iwamura. – 1st ed. p. cm.
Added t.p. title: Doko e iku no? Tomodachi ni ai ni!.
ISBN: 0-439-41659-0
Title: Doko e iku no? Tomodachi ni ai ni!. II. Iwamura, Kazuo, 1939- III. Title.
PL853.W335 D65 2003
495.6'86421—dc21
2002070396
10 9 8 7 6 5 4 3 2   03 04 05 06 07

Printed in Malaysia 46
Reinforced Binding for Library Use
First Scholastic edition, April 2003

Eric Carle & Kazuo Iwamura

Where Are You Going? To See My Friend!

Orchard Books / New York AN IMPRINT OF SCHOLASTIC INC.

Where are you going?

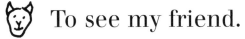 To see my friend.

 What is your friend like?

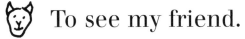 A good singer

I like singing, too.
Meow Meow Meow
May I come with you?

Yes, come along.
My friend is your friend.

Where are you going?

 To see my friend.

 What is your friend like?

 A good singer

I like singing, too.
Cock a doodle doo
May I come with you?

 Yes, come along.
Our friend is your friend.

Where are you going?

 To see my friend.

 What is your friend like?

 A good singer

I like singing, too.
Baa Baa Baa
May I come with you?

Yes, come along.
Our friend is your friend.

Where are you going?

To see my friend.

What is your friend like?

A good singer

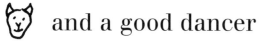 and a good dancer

I like dancing, too.
Hop Hop Hop
May I come with you?

Yes, come along.
Our friend is your friend.

Hop Hop Hop

Baa Baa Baa

Cock a doodle doo

Meow Meow Meow

Bow Wow Wow

Hop Hop Hop

 Baa Baa Baa

 Cock a doodle doo

Meow Meow Meow

Bow Wow Wow
These are my Friends.

 Wonderful!
Your friends are my friends, too.
You are good singers and good dancers!

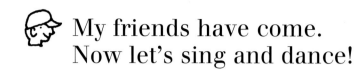 My friends have come.
Now let's sing and dance!

わたしの　ともだちが　きたよ。
wa ta she no　toe mo da chi ga　kee ta yo

さあ、うたお！
sa ah uh ta oh ！

さあ、おどろ！
sa ah oh doe ro ！

ワン ワン ワン
wan wan wan

みんな ぼくの
min na bo ku no

ともだちだよ。
toe mo da chi da yo

わーい！
wah ee !

あなたの ともだちは
ah na ta no toe mo da chi wa

わたしの ともだちよ。
wa ta she no toe mo da chi yo

みんな うたが うまいし
min na uu ta ga uu ma ee she

ダンスも じょうず。
dan su mo jo uu zu

どんな　ともだち？

うたが　うまいんだ。

ダンスも　じょうず。

ダンスなら　ぼくも　だいすき。

タッ　タッ　タッ

ぼくも　あいたいな。

いいとも。

ぼくらの　ともだちは

きみの　ともだちさ。

どこへ　いくの？

doe ko eh　ee ku no ?

ともだちに
あいに！

toe mo da chi ni
ah ee ni !

いいとも。
ぼくらの ともだちは
きみの ともだちさ。

ee ee toe mo
bo ku ra no toe mo da chi wa
kee mi no toe mo da chi sa

うたなら ぼくも だいすき。
メエー メエー メエー
ぼくも あいたいな。

uu ta na ra bo ku mo da ee su kee
meh meh meh
bo ku mo ah ee ta ee na

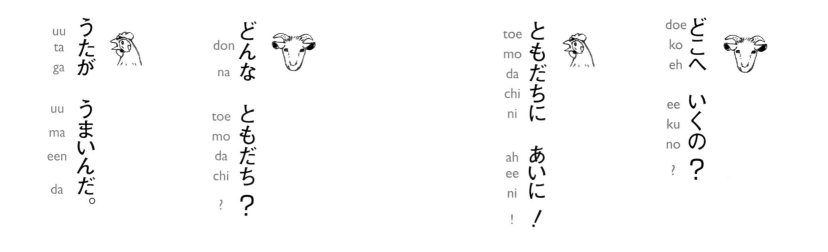

どこへ いくの？
doe ko eh ee ku no ?

ともだちに あいに！
toe mo da chi ni ah ee ni !

どんな ともだち？
don na toe mo da chi ?

うたが うまいんだ。
uu ta ga uu ma een da

いいとも。
ぼくらの　ともだちは
きみの　ともだちさ。

ee ee toe mo
bo ku ra no toe mo da chi wa
kee mi no toe mo da chi sa

うたなら　わたしも　だいすき。
コッ　コッ　コケーコ
わたしも　あいたいな。

uu ta na ra wa ta she mo da ee su kee
kok kok ko keh ko
wa ta she mo ah ee ta ee na

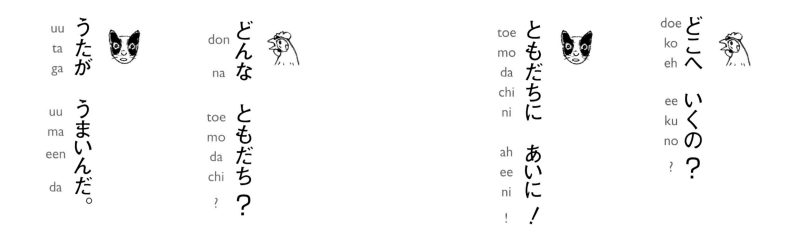

どこへ　いくの？
doe ko eh　ee ku no ？

ともだちに　あいに！
toe mo da chi ni　ah ee ni ！

どんな　ともだち？
don na　toe mo da chi ？

うたが　うまいんだ。
uu ta ga　uu ma een da

うたなら わたしも だいすき。

ニャオ ニャオ ニャオ

わたしも あいたいな。

いいとも。

ぼくの ともだちは

きみの ともだちさ。

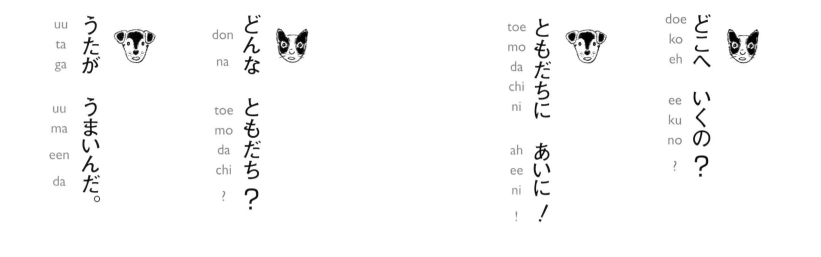

どこへ　いくの？
doeko eh　eekuno ?

ともだちに　あいに！
toemodachini　ahee ni !

どんな　ともだち？
donna　toemodachi ?

うたが　うまいんだ。
uutaga　uumaeen da

どこへ
_{doe ko eh}

いくの？
_{ee ku no ?}

ともだちに
_{toe mo da chi ni}

あいに！
_{ah ee ni !}

エリック・カール

いわむら かずお

ニューヨーク

スカラスティック社　オーチャード・ブックス部門

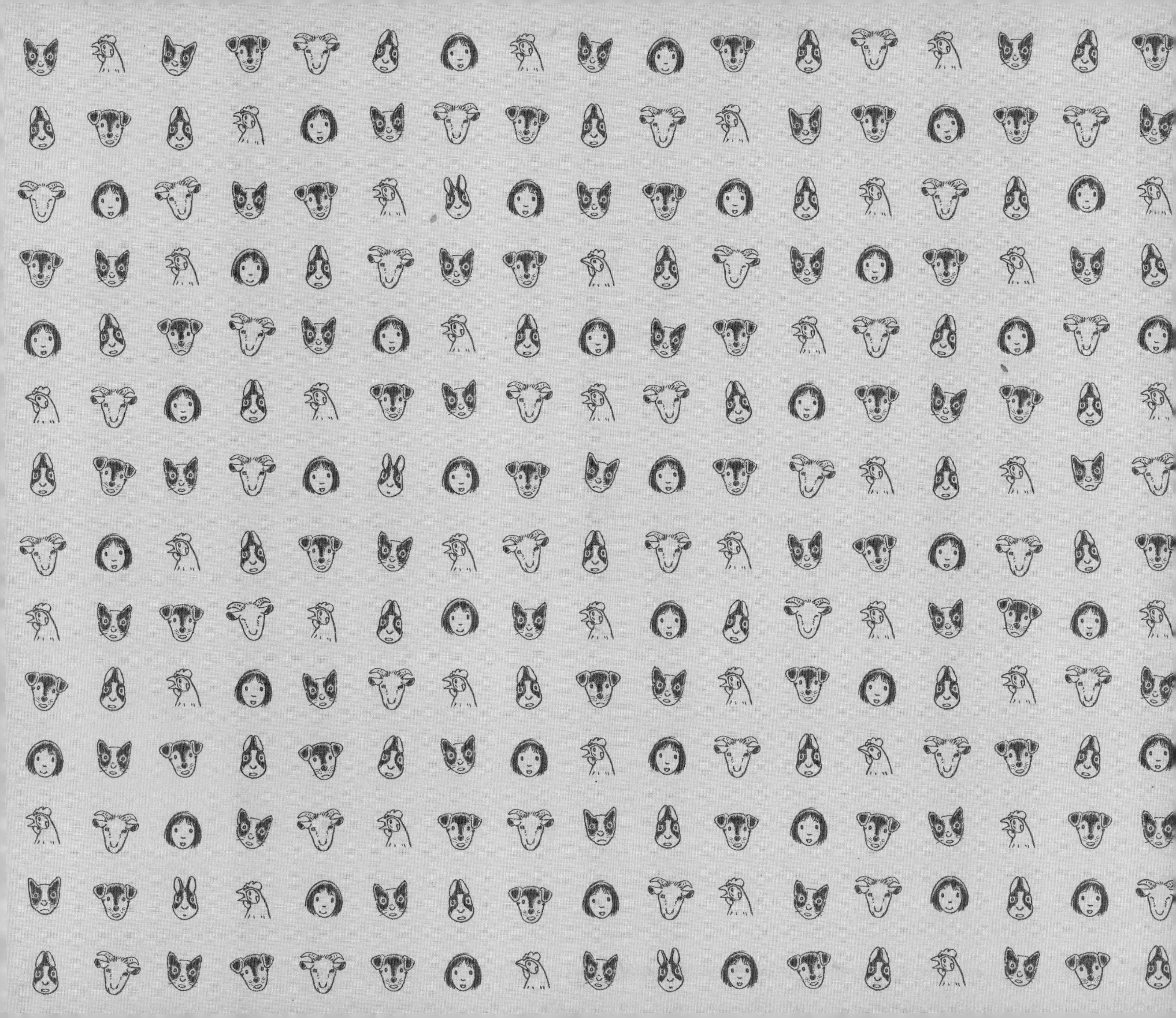